SOMETIMES I'M A PILLOW

"Sometimes I'm a pillow"

Written by Susan Lovett
Illustrated by Larisa ivankovic

HI! MY NAME IS KAI,

AND I'M A KID.
I'M ALSO A PILLOW, A PORCUPINE,
A RIVER, A HAMMER, A NOODLE,
A STONE, A SKATEBOARD,
A MOUSE AND A TREE.

I CAN BE AND FEEL A LOT OF THINGS,
AND ALL OF THEM ARE PARTS OF ME.

WHEN I'M A PILLOW,

I FEEL CUDDLY AND SOFT AND I LIKE TO GIVE HUGS.
I CAN BE A PILLOW WHEN PEOPLE ARE NICE TO ME.
SOMETIMES I'M A PILLOW FOR NO REASON AT ALL.

DO YOU EVER FEEL CUDDLY - LIKE A PILLOW?

WHEN I'M A HAMMER,

I JUST WANT TO SMASH AND CRASH. I GET LOUD.
I CAN BE A HAMMER WHEN EVERYTHING'S
GOING WRONG FOR ME.
SOMETIMES I'M A HAMMER JUST BECAUSE.

DO YOU EVER FEEL ANGRY - LIKE A HAMMER?

WHEN I'M A RIVER,

I FEEL PEACEFUL AND RELAXED. NOTHING BOTHERS ME.
I CAN BE A RIVER WHEN I'M AROUND PEOPLE I REALLY LIKE.
SOMETIMES I'M A RIVER FOR NO SPECIAL REASON.

DO YOU EVER FEEL CALM - LIKE A RIVER?

WHEN I'M A PORCUPINE,

I DON'T WANT TO TALK TO ANYBODY.
I GET QUIET AND PRICKLY. I CAN BE A PORCUPINE
WHEN I WANT EVERYONE TO JUST LEAVE ME ALONE.
SOMETIMES I DON'T EVEN KNOW WHY I'M A PORCUPINE.
DO YOU EVER FEEL GROUCHY - LIKE A PORCUPINE?

WHEN I'M A SKATEBOARD,

I HAVE A LOT OF ENERGY. I NEED TO MOVE REALLY FAST.
I CAN BE A SKATEBOARD WHEN THERE'S
A LOT GOING ON IN MY BRAIN.
SOMETIMES I JUST WAKE UP
WITH EXTRA SKATEBOARD MOTION.

DO YOU EVER FEEL EXCITED - LIKE A SKATEBOARD?

WHEN I'M A STONE,

I FEEL HEAVY AND ALL ALONE.

I CAN BE A STONE WHEN MY FEELINGS GET HURT.

SOMETIMES I FEEL LIKE A STONE AND I DON'T CARE.

DO YOU EVER FEEL SAD - LIKE A STONE?

WHEN I'M A NOODLE,

I'M FLOPPY AND FUNNY.

I CAN BE A NOODLE WHEN I CAN'T STOP GIGGLING.

SOMETIME'S I'M A NOODLE WHEN I'M AROUND OTHER NOODLES.

DO YOU EVER FEEL SILLY - LIKE A NOODLE?

WHEN I'M A MOUSE,

I FEEL WORRIED AND SMALL.

I CAN BE A MOUSE WHEN PEOPLE ARE SHOUTING OR FIGHTING.

SOMETIMES I'M A MOUSE BUT I'M NOT SURE WHY.

DO YOU EVER FEEL NERVOUS - LIKE A MOUSE?

WHEN I'M A TREE,

I FEEL STRONG AND PROUD. I'M GROWING UP.
I CAN BE A TREE WHEN I'VE DONE SOMETHING GOOD
AND I'M HAPPY TO BE ME.
SOMETIMES I'M NOT SURE WHAT MAKES ME A TREE.

DO YOU EVER FEEL HAPPY - LIKE A TREE?

I'M KAI AND I'M A KID.

MY FEELINGS CAN CHANGE ME
INTO OTHER THINGS, TOO.

HOW DO YOUR FEELINGS SOMETIMES CHANGE YOU?

ABOUT THE AUTHOR

Susan Lovett is a licensed clinical social worker and certified classroom teacher who has worked with low-income youth and families in Boston for over 20 years. Susan is the founder and director of **Hands to Heart Center - Yoga for the People**, a nonprofit organization that shares the healing practices of yoga and mindfulness with people affected by addiction, poverty and trauma.

She was inspired to write "Sometimes I'm a Pillow" by the many wonderful children she has worked with and learned from in her social work career.